Katie Morag
and the New Pier

Happy Christmas 2015

Best Wishes
Friends of Green Hammerton Primary School

To the old ways – and the new

KATIE MORAG AND THE NEW PIER
A RED FOX BOOK 978 1 782 95619 8

First published in Great Britain by The Bodley Head,
an imprint of Random House Children's Publishers UK
A Random House Group Company

The Bodley Head edition published 1993
Red Fox edition published 1997
This Red Fox edition published 2015

1 3 5 7 9 10 8 6 4 2

Red Fox Books are published by Random House Children's Publishers UK,
61–63 Uxbridge Road, London W5 5SA

www.randomhousechildrens.co.uk
www.randomhouse.co.uk

Addresses for companies within The Random House Group Limited can be found at:
www.randomhouse.co.uk/offices.htm

THE RANDOM HOUSE GROUP Limited Reg. No. 954009

A CIP catalogue record for this book is available from the British Library.

Printed in China

Penguin Random House is committed to a sustainable future for our business, our readers
and our planet. This book is made from Forest Stewardship Council® certified paper.

Katie Morag
and the New Pier

Mairi Hedderwick

RED FOX

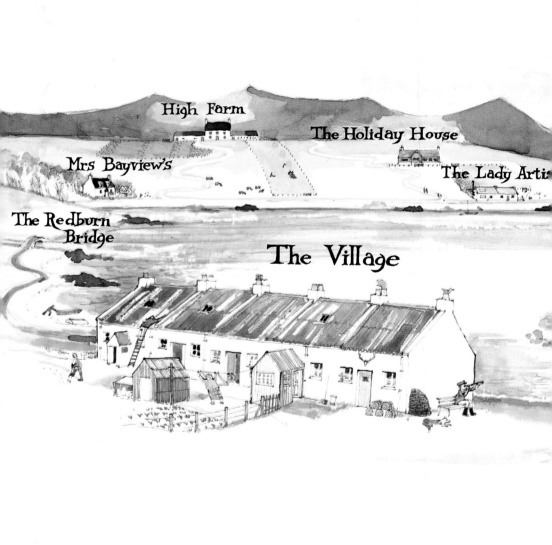

High Farm

The Holiday House

Mrs Bayview's

The Lady Arti

The Redburn
Bridge

The Village

THE ISLE of STRUAY

Grannie's

The Mainland

The Jetty

ISLE of STRUAY
SHOP & POST OFFICE

OBAN
TIMES
GET
YOUR COPY
HERE

The Shop & Post Office

For months workmen had been
building a new pier on the Isle
of Struay. They were a cheery lot
and lived in huts by the shore.
They only complained when the
weather got too bad to get on with

the work; they felt homesick for
their families and friends on the
mainland.

They looked forward to the day
the new pier would be finished. So
did the islanders.

Katie Morag was especially excited about the new pier.

"The boat will be able to come to Struay THREE times a week instead of one," said her father, Mr McColl, the shopkeeper.

Mrs McColl, the postmistress, was delighted. She would have lots more mail deliveries to do.

"Grandma Mainland will be able to come more often," said Neilly Beag.

"And she will be able to get away quicker," said Grannie Island, who was not very sure about the new pier but saw that it had some advantages.

But for the most part Grannie Island was pessimistic.

"The old ways will be forgotten," she frowned. "The place will get too busy; there will be no more jaunts out in the ferryboat to the big boat in the Bay."

Grannie Island often manned the ferryboat on the days when the ferryman was ill or on holiday. "I'll miss that. And so will you, Katie Morag. And what will the ferryman do for a living?" Katie Morag hadn't thought about all that.

In the village people
were saying it was time
the old ways changed.
They started to paint their
windows and gates bright colours
and tidy their gardens. Mrs Baxter
said she was going to open up
a Craft Shop. The Lady Artist,
of course, was already making
interesting things to sell in it.

On the other side of the Bay
Mr MacMaster, the farmer, was
very pleased. "I'll be able to send
off eggs, milk and cheese to the
mainland THREE times a week!"

"Ach well," sighed the ferryman,
"I suppose I'll soon be redundant."

"What does that mean?" asked
Katie Morag.

"No longer wanted," replied the
ferryman as he and Katie Morag
walked along the shore. Katie
Morag nearly tripped over a large,

blue, neatly coiled rope on the tideline.

"Finders keepers," said the ferryman. "That's the rule of the sea when something is washed up on the tide."

"Oh no – I'll give it to the ferryboat," declared Katie Morag.

"Have you been having the
ferryman's wife's chocolate cake
again?" asked Mrs McColl crossly,
as Katie Morag toyed with her tea
that night. She had, but it wasn't the
cake that was making Katie Morag
sad.

She tried to tell Mr and Mrs McColl
all about the ferryman but her parents
were not listening.

"The pier will be finished by the
spring, weather permitting," said Mrs
McColl, looking at the calendar.

Spring came but it
did not come alone.
It was accompanied
by fearsome storms. One especially
wet and windy day the foreman on
the pier told the men to tie down the
equipment and stop work. It was
boring sitting in the huts waiting
for the wild weather to end, so the

workmen visited the
islanders, and sat
by their cosy fires
and told stories about life on the
mainland.

Jimmy and George were in the
McColls' kitchen when the foreman
burst in. "The huts are floating out
to sea!" he shouted.

Everyone rushed to the door
and sure enough there was the
new pier awash, but not a
hut in sight save one that
bobbed and bucked in the
Bay. The rest had all sunk.

There was something else bobbing
in the Bay. It was the ferryboat!
Katie Morag could just make out
the ferryman throwing a rope over
the handle of the hut door. But as
Grannie Island steered the ferryboat
alongside, a huge wave lifted the

rope off the handle and the hut
started to drift out to sea again.

"Use my rope!" shouted Katie
Morag at the top of her voice.

Grannie Island revved the boat close to the hut again and as she circled round it so went the strong blue rope.

Everyone cheered as the ferryboat towed the hut to the shore.

"What seamanship!" said the workmen. "What a rope!" said the ferryman, smiling at Katie Morag as he stepped out of the boat.

"You can't sleep in that!" said the islanders as sodden mattresses and broken bits of furniture fell out of the hut door.

"You will just have to stay with us until the new pier is finished."

"Great!" thought Katie Morag. "Mainland stories every night!"

Next morning the storm had
subsided and the men went back
to work. The foreman said the
ferryman could keep the hut for
firewood. He and the men thought it
was just fine staying in the islanders'
homes – much more comfortable
than the huts.

Each workman boasted that his lodgings were the best but everyone had to agree that the ferryman's wife's chocolate cake was quite the most fabbydoo.

It was Easter and the new pier was
finally completed. The boat came
alongside laden with important
people and visitors. And there was
Grandma Mainland! The workmen
shook hands with the islanders and
said they would be back for their

holidays. Nearly everyone wanted to book in at the ferryman's house and Katie Morag knew why.

"That's it, then," sighed Grannie Island as hordes of visitors meandered towards the village. "The end of the ferryboat and the old ways."

"No, it is not!" said Katie Morag, taking her two grandmothers over to the ferryman's house. The hut was transformed: inside, a counter displayed several chocolate cakes and pots of tea. Grandma Mainland was first in the queue.

"After the visitors have had their tea, you and I and Katie Morag

can take them out for a jaunt in
the ferryboat, Grannie Island,"
suggested the ferryman.

"And you can tell them all about
the old ways," said Katie Morag.

Grannie Island smiled. The new
pier was not going to be such a bad
thing after all.